Extreme Science

by David Orme

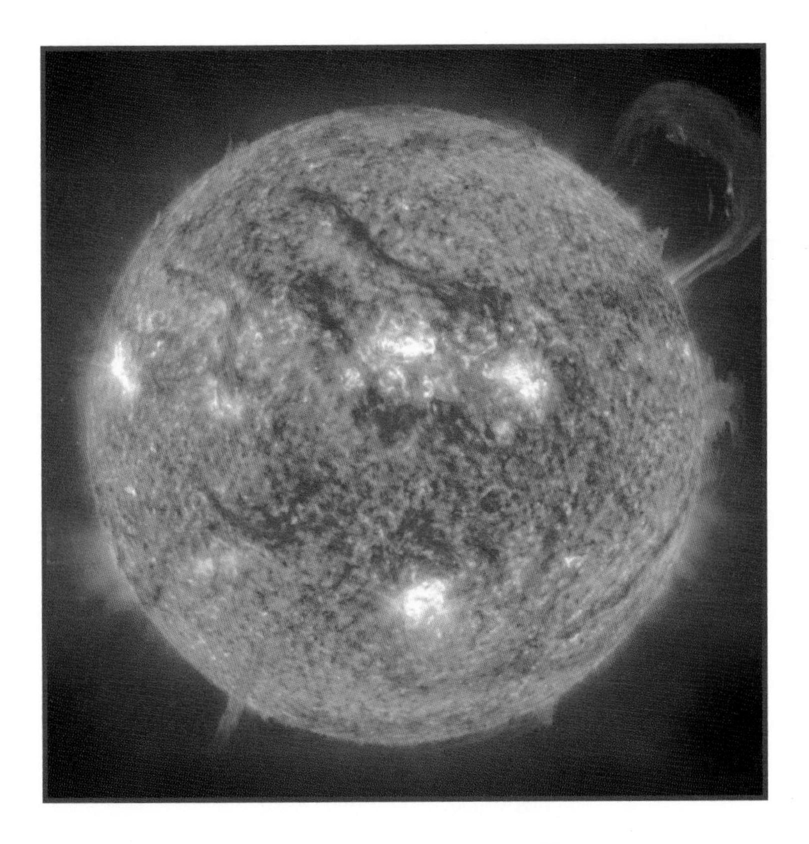

Perfection Learning®

Extreme Science

by David Orme

Educational consultant: Helen Bird

Illustrated by Neil Smith

Image Credits

'Get the Facts' section - images copyright: police box - Malcolm Romain; clock background - Emin Aykut; robot hand - Konstantin Inozemtsev; fruit fly - arlindo71; nanobots - Michael Knight; granny - bobbieo; gravity vortex - Terraxplorer; apple - Joanna Pecha; dinosaur - illustrated by Cyber Media (India) Ltd., copyright Ransom Publishing Ltd.; Sun, Earth and infant stars in the Small Magellanic Cloud courtesy NASA Jet Propulsion Laboratory (NASA-JPL); party girl - Bulent Ince; DNA - Kirsty Pargeter; refuse bin - Skip O'Donnell; technician - Kenn Wislande; brain mechanism - Vasiliy Yakobchuk; cyberface - Antonis Papantoniou; big bang -Jamie Shields; grumpy penguin - Dean Murray; weighing scales - Julie Felton; space rocket Mark Stay; worm - Gary Daniels.

First published in 2008

This edition is published by arrangement with Ransom Publishing Ltd.
First American edition 2009

Printed in the United States of America

Perfection Learning® Corporation
1000 North Second Avenue
P.O. Box 500
Logan, Iowa 51546-0500
Tel: 1-800-831-4190 • Fax: 1-800-543-2745
perfectionlearning.com

1 2 3 4 5 6 7 PP 14 13 12 11 10 09

RLB ISBN-13: 978-0-7569-9279-8
RLB ISBN-10: 0-7569-9279-6

PB ISBN-13: 978-0-7891-7902-9
PB ISBN-10: 0-7891-7902-4

Table of Contents

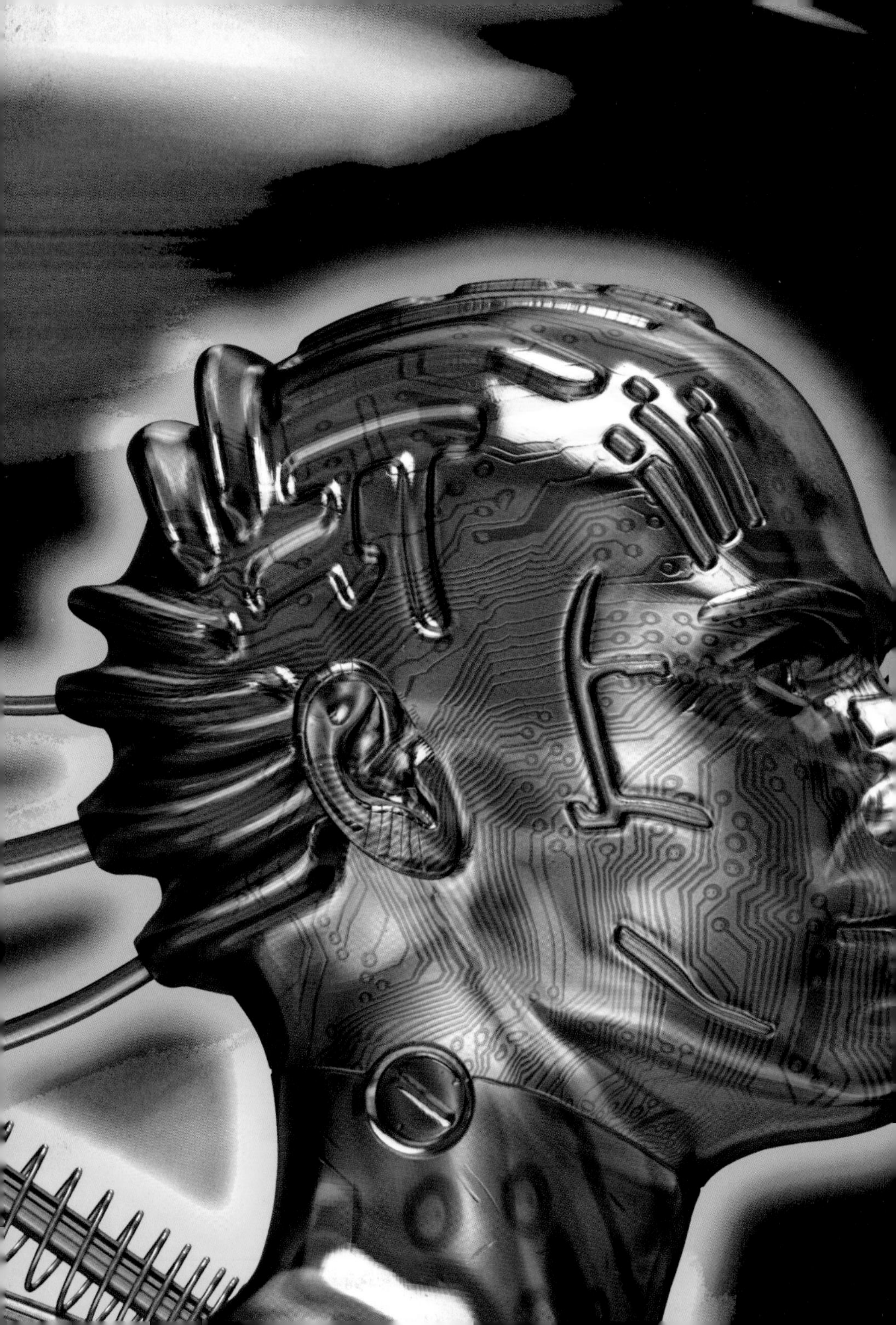

Get the facts

Beginnings and endings

How did the universe start?

Most scientists say the universe started with a **big bang** 13.7 billion years ago.

How do they know?

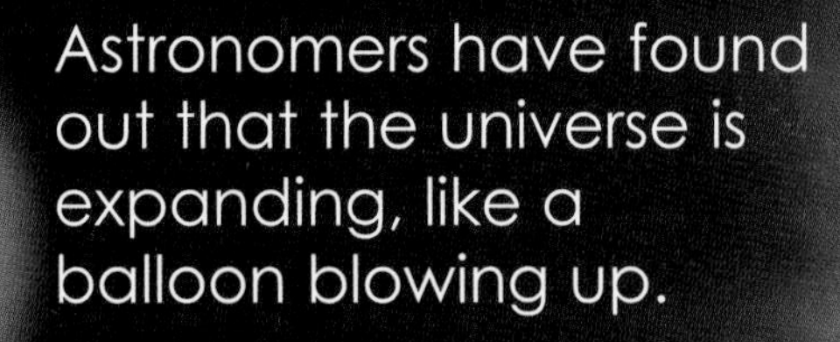

Astronomers have found out that the universe is expanding, like a balloon blowing up.

They know how fast this is happening.

This means they can work out when the universe was very tiny and very hot.

What made the bang?

No one really knows.

It could be that when the universe is as big as it can get, it will start to shrink back down to a point again. (This is sometimes called "**the big crunch**.")

Another big bang will happen, and a new universe will start. This will happen over and over.

So when will our universe end?

Some scientists say it will expand forever and there won't be a big crunch. The problem will be that the heat in the universe will be spread so thinly that everything will die— **the big freeze**.

What will happen after the end of the universe?

We'll just have to wait and see!

Here's another idea:

Maybe there are other universes, only we can't see them because they are in a different dimension.

Our universe started when two other universes touched each other.

Will we ever visit the stars?

The **nearest star** is our sun. The next star is a very long way away. It takes more than four years for its light to reach the Earth.

Light travels at **670 million miles per hour**. The space shuttle at top speed would take 160,000 years to get there!

But what if we traveled faster than light?

Albert Einstein said that **nothing** can travel faster than light. If you tried, very odd things would happen.

The nearer you get to the speed of light, the more **energy** you need to go even faster. You would be getting heavier and heavier!

As you go faster, time moves more slowly compared to Earth time.

If you were traveling at nearly the speed of light a person on Earth would think your clock had stopped.

What about space warps and wormholes?

People think it might be possible to take a **shortcut** through space.

Imagine that space is a sheet of paper with two points on it. To get from one point to the other you could:

- walk along the paper from one to the other. For a tiny creature, this would take a long time.
- fold the piece of paper so the points are next to each other (**a space warp**).
- bend the piece of paper over something round, like an apple, then make a tunnel through the apple (**a wormhole**).

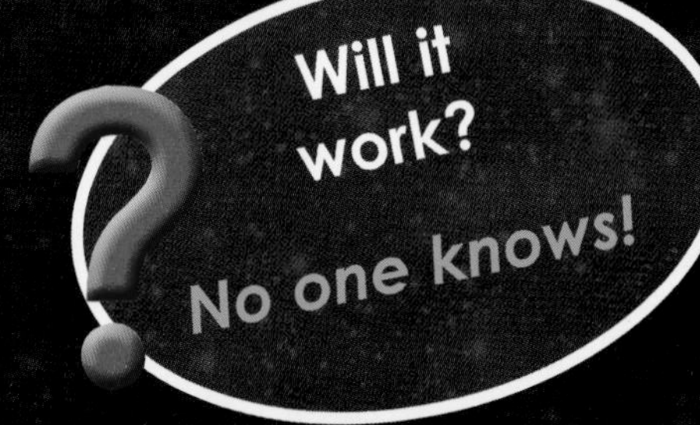

Time travel

Time travel makes great stories, but ***could it happen***?

Scientists say it is possible, but they don't know how to make a machine to do it.

How would it work?

1 Going really fast

If you traveled at nearly the **speed of light**, your watch would slow down compared to watches on Earth. You wouldn't notice it, though, because you would **slow down** as well.

One year on a spaceship traveling near the speed of light . . .

might get you back to Earth hundreds of years in the future!

2 A wormhole time machine

A wormhole can be a time machine

A **wormhole** is a shortcut from one **place** to another. A special wormhole can also be a shortcut from one **time** to another.

Start by making one end of the wormhole faster or slower than the other.

Then go through the wormhole. You will end up in the past or the future.

EASY!

Be careful if you go into the past. Don't change anything! Even a small change will affect your own time.

Bringing dinosaurs to life

Jurassic Park was a great movie. But could you really bring dinosaurs to life?

How would it work?

A living thing's genes are a set of instructions, or a pattern. Our genes, called our DNA, mean that we turn out as a human being, not an elephant or a slug.

Our DNA is in every cell of our body.

DNA

?

If we could find dinosaur DNA, we could

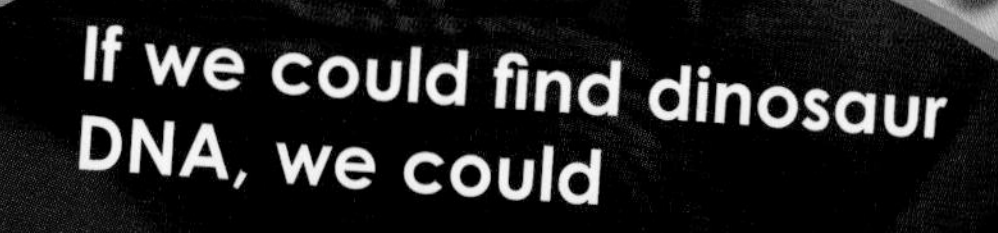

take the DNA out of an animal egg,

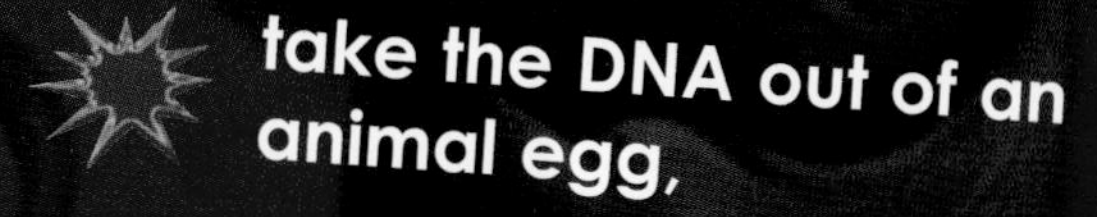

put the dinosaur DNA in instead,

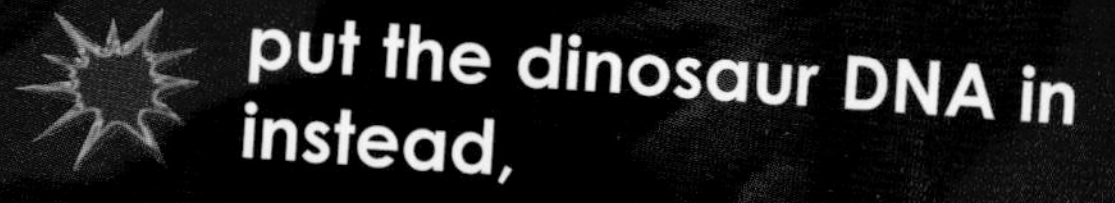

wait for it to grow.

Then stand back!

Would it work?

Er . . . probably not. You would need all the DNA, and that is very long and complicated. It would be impossible to find this after millions of years.

So that's it, then?

NOT QUITE

It might work for other extinct animals.

Scientists in Russia have found the bodies of mammoths frozen in ice. The DNA might be complete! You could use modern elephants as mothers.

Intelligent machines

Look at this notice:

What does it mean?

Put garbage here

Maybe this picture will help:

Computers are **smart**. They can beat you at chess and add up numbers millions of times faster than you can. They can store a huge amount of stuff in their memory.

The trouble is, apart from being smart, they are also **stupid**. They wouldn't be able to work out what the notice meant.

Here are two jokes.

Why do seagulls fly over the sea?

Because if they flew over the bay, they would be bagels!

Why was 6 afraid of 7?

Because 789!

No computer has yet been made that could get these jokes.

ho ho ho ho

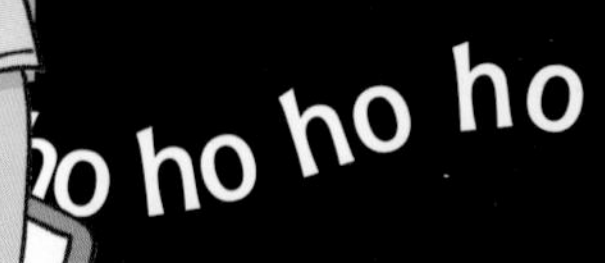

Intelligence isn't just about doing things quickly.

It's about using your **experiences** of the world to help you work things out.

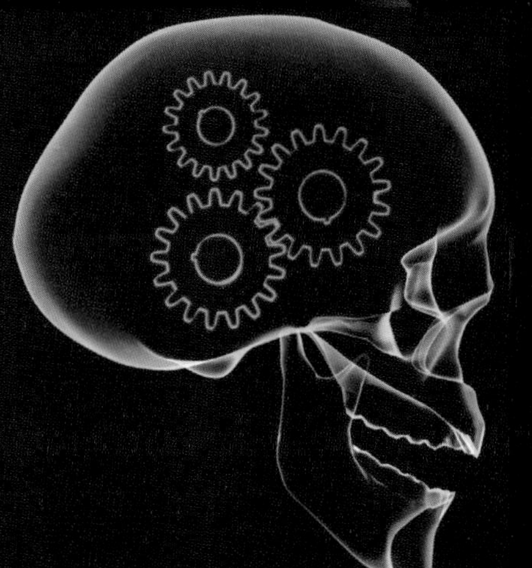

A machine that could do this probably wouldn't be made of metal and silicon chips.

It would have to be made of something that could learn and grow by itself.

In the future there may be artificial brains that can think like we do.

Maybe they could even understand these jokes.

But what might happen if they ended up cleverer than we are?

Could we live forever?

The **cells** in our bodies replace themselves by dividing.

As we get older, this doesn't work so well. Our bodies start to **wear out**. It seems our bodies are designed to do this.

Scientists think they may be able to stop this from happening by changing our **DNA**.

They have already made **fruit flies** live twice as long as normal.

They are looking at human **stem cells**. These could be used to repair any part of our body.

Another idea is to use **nanobots**.

A nanobot

These are **tiny machines** the size of **molecules**.

They would live inside us, repairing damage and destroying things like cancer cells.

But we might still be killed in an accident.

So here's another idea.

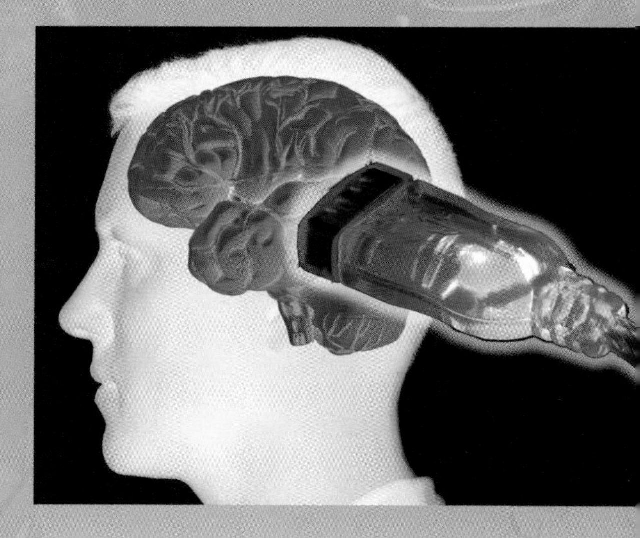

Some people say we could add **extra parts** to our brain.

We could have a much **bigger memory** and wouldn't forget things. We could work things out much more quickly. We could even have an online connection to the **Internet** in our heads.

Maybe, if we could do that, we could have an **artificial body** too. If it wore out, we could buy a new one.

Or maybe we don't need a body at all . . .

But would it still be us?

What do you think?

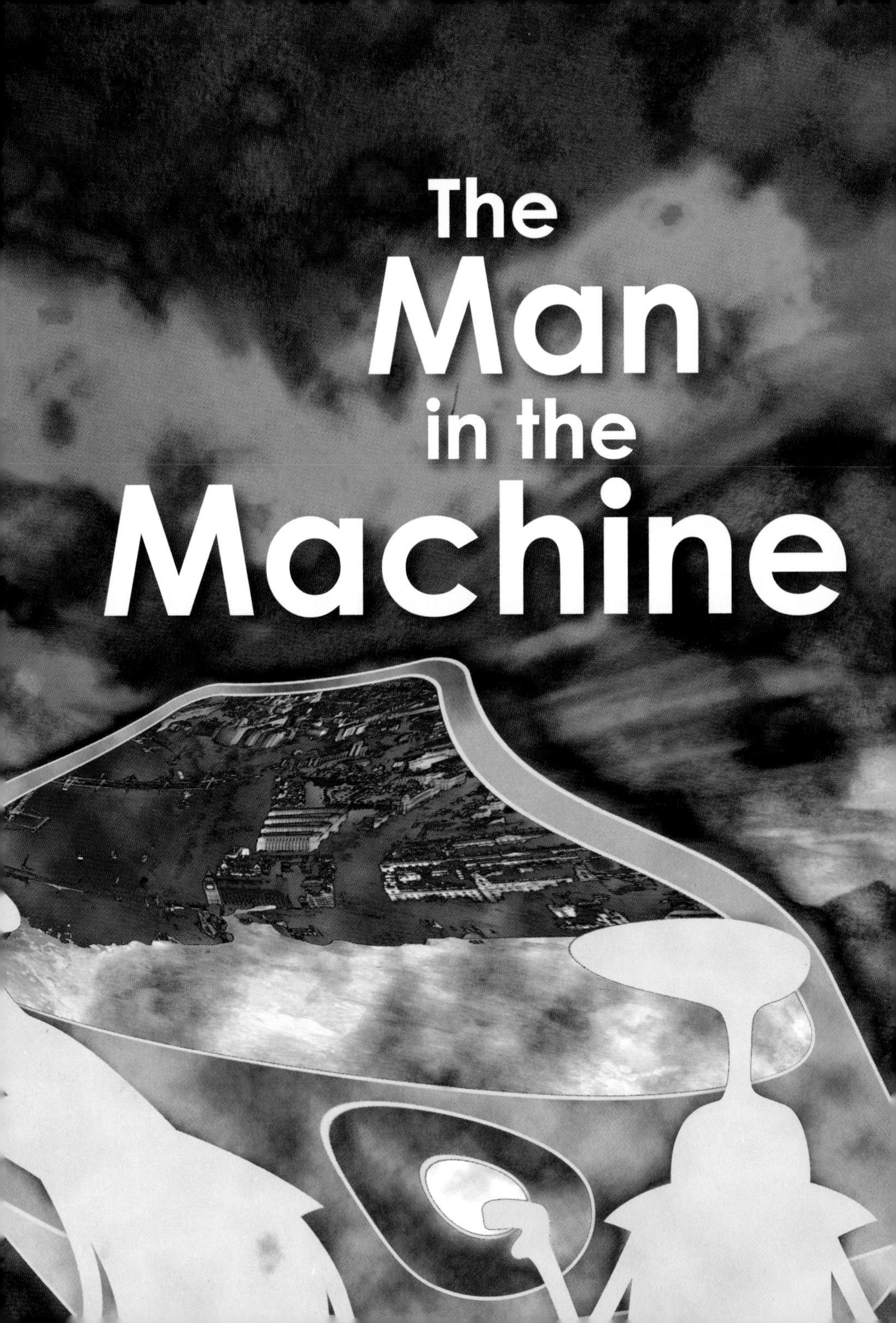
The Man in the Machine

Chapter 1
The world in the computer

Two alien scientists stared at the machine.

"This is the most powerful computer ever," said 4 Square. "It has a complete universe in its memory. Look!"

The other scientist stared at a screen. He saw galaxies and stars swirling in space.

4 Square pressed a button. It looked like they were traveling through space. On and on, until they got to a small sun.

Somewhere on a distant planet...
This is the most powerful computer ever. It has a complete universe in its memory!

They saw a green and blue planet. There were mountains and forests and great cities full of people.

"All those people think they are real and live in a real world!" said 4 Square.

"They don't know that my computer made them all this morning—and put a history of thousands of years into their heads!"

All these people think they are real. But the computer made them all this morning and put their history into their heads!

Chapter 2
"I can control everything!"

"What are you going to do with your computer world?" asked 2 Ring, the other scientist.

"I'm bored with it already. I'll turn it off this afternoon."

"But that's terrible! What about all those people?"

"But they're not real! Look, I can control everything!"

What are you going to do with your computer world?
I'm bored with it. I'm going to turn it off this afternoon.
But that's terrible! All those people!

2 Ring watched in horror as 4 Square created a flood and made a wall of water crash into a city.

"You can play if you like," said 4 Square. "I'm off to make something even better!"

When 4 Square had gone, 2 Ring sat down at the computer. These people may be in a machine, but their thoughts were real.

He had to save at least one of them!

But they're not real! Look, I'll make a flood crash into that city. You can play if you like.

I must save at least one of those people.

Chapter 3
The alien in the woods

Jamie Banks had had a hard day at school. He had just taken his first exam, and he didn't think he had done well. And there was a whole week of exams to come!

He plodded along a path through the woods. He had come here because it was quiet.

Suddenly, a very weird creature was standing in front of him.

"Hi," said Jamie. "Love the costume."

Jamie Banks is on his way home . . .
Hi! Love the costume!

"I am a scientist from another world—the real world. You are just part of a computer program! And it will be switched off at five o'clock this afternoon!"

"Yeah, right," said Jamie. "What's this, some crazy TV show?"

2 Ring did not argue. He grabbed Jamie's arm.

For Jamie, the world disappeared.

You are just part of a computer program, and it will be switched off this afternoon!
Yeah, right! What's this, a crazy TV show?
But the scientist did not have time to argue . . .

Chapter 4
The great turn-off

"So let's get this straight," said Jamie. "My universe is just a computer program invented by this 4 Square person?"

"That is so. 4 Square is clever, but so am I. I have re-created your body here in the real world."

"But what about my world?"

"All gone, I'm afraid. 4 Square switched it off this afternoon."

"Well, at least there'll be no more exams. But what am I going to do in this world? I'm not a clever scientist like you."

"I don't know. But we'll think of something!"

So my universe was just a computer program?
Yes, and it's just been switched off!
But what am I going to do in this world? I'm not a clever scientist!
We'll think of something!

In a great glass building on top of a mountain, two scientists looked at a screen.

"That's amazing! In the universe you made in your computer, someone was clever enough to do the same thing and make a universe of their own!"

"That's right! And another scientist rescued someone from that world before it was shut down!"

"Shall we rescue someone in the same way?"

"No, bad idea. As that young man said, what would they do in our world—the real world?"

With a flick of a switch the scientist turned off the computer.

So in the universe you made in your computer, someone was clever enough to do the same thing.
Yes! And he rescued someone from the program before it was shut down!
Shall we rescue someone in the same way?
Bad idea. What could they do in our world?
With a flick of a switch, the scientist turned off the computer.

Extreme Science word check

artificial
astronomer
computer
dimension
dinosaur
DNA
energy
galaxy
genes
mammoth
molecules
nanobots
program
scientist
silicon chips
space shuttle
stem cells
universe
wormhole